Discard.

JOSEPHINE'S
DREAM

Acknowledgements

Many thanks to Tim Robinson and Britney Rule

Dedication

For Wendy Singh, Eleanor Narod, Anne Andrew, and Judy Growe—and, of course, Tom and Dov.

Silverleaf Press Books are available exclusively through
Independent Publishers Group.

For details write or telephone
Independent Publishers Group, 814 North Franklin St.
Chicago, IL 60610, (312) 337-0747

Silverleaf Press
8160 South Highland Drive
Sandy, Utah 84093

JOSEPHINE'S DREAM

Written by Joan Betty Stuchner
Illustrated by Chantelle Walther

SILVERLEAF
PRESS

JOSEPHINE BAKER STARTED life as Josephine Freda Carson in St. Louis, Missouri.

She was poor in money but rich in talent. Even as a child she sang, danced, crossed her eyes, knocked her knees, and made crazy funny faces. Her parents were performers and the theater was in her blood.

But Josephine's parents had a hard time making a living. In 1906, the year of Josephine's birth, it wasn't so easy to make any kind of living, especially if you were black and living in East St. Louis.

JOSE

When Josephine was a little girl she had to go out to work. She cleaned houses and took care of other people's children, even though she was only a child herself.

The families she worked for were not always kind to Josephine. But Josephine had a dream.

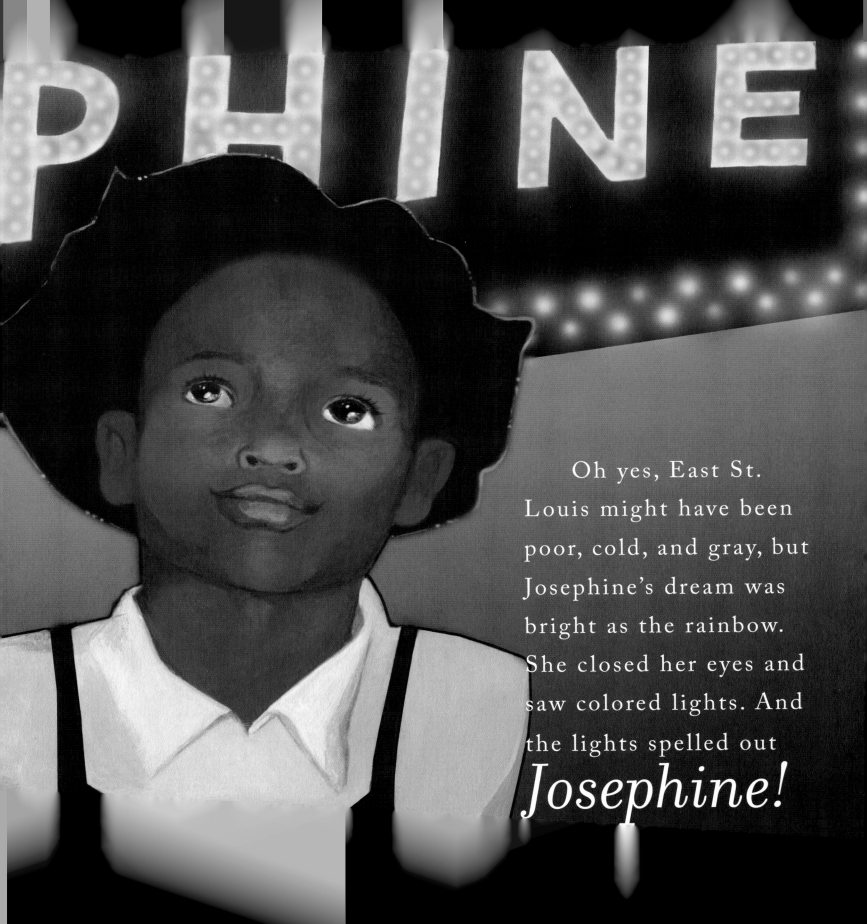

Oh yes, East St. Louis might have been poor, cold, and gray, but Josephine's dream was bright as the rainbow. She closed her eyes and saw colored lights. And the lights spelled out *Josephine!*

When she was thirteen, Josephine waited tables in a café. Of course, being Josephine, she didn't just serve food to the customers. She served entertainment, too.

She sang, danced, crossed her eyes and knocked her knees, and made crazy funny faces. The customers went wild.

"Encore," they cried, "encore!"

Josephine's schoolteachers were not her biggest fans.

They were enraged when she stood in front of the class, crossed her eyes, knocked her knees, and pulled her crazy funny faces.

They didn't shout, "Encore, Josephine, encore!"

They sent her to the principal's office instead.

One day a band of street musicians, the Jones Family, said, "Josephine, you are so talented. Why not join us?" She did.

Performing was much more fun than cleaning houses and waiting tables or going to school.

The Jones Family entertained customers lining up to get into a vaudeville theater. Josephine sang, danced, crossed her eyes, knocked her knees, and pulled crazy funny faces.

The people in the lineups went wild. "Encore, Josephine," they cried, "encore!"

The theater manager took note. He invited the Jones Family to perform on the stage instead of in the street. Little Josephine became a big hit.

Josephine Carson became Josephine Baker. Even though her name wasn't in lights yet, she always stole the show. But she soon figured out that it wasn't going to be easy for a black performer to see her name in lights.

Not in America. Not in the 1920s.

It was time to pack her bags and cross the Atlantic Ocean. Oh yes, Josephine still had that bright rainbow dream. She closed her eyes and saw herself performing on stage in glittering costumes. The dazzled audience cried, "Encore, Josephine, encore!"

Josephine went all the way to Paris, France. Soon she was performing to packed houses at the Follies-Bergere. The Parisians loved her. They loved her songs, they loved her dances, and they loved her crazy funny faces. They applauded, laughed, and shouted, "Encore, Josephine, encore!"

At night the marquee lights of Paris twinkled and glittered brighter than the stars in the sky. Josephine loved Paris. She loved the applause, the laughter, and the shouts of, "Encore, Josephine, encore!"

At last the name that lit up the marquee in brightly colored rainbow lights was JOSEPHINE BAKER. Life was good. Josephine's dream had come true.

"If only other children's dreams could come true," she said.

But then one day the lights of Paris went out.
Everything was dark.

Enemy soldiers marched into France. "We don't like lights," the soldiers declared.

Cannons fired. Smoke filled the sky.

Josephine was sad, but she still danced. She still sang. She still made crazy funny faces. The Parisians applauded, laughed, and shouted, "Encore, Josephine, encore!" Josephine helped them forget the soldiers.

She helped in other ways, too, because Josephine wasn't only talented, she was also brave. She secretly worked with the French Resistance to get rid of the enemy.

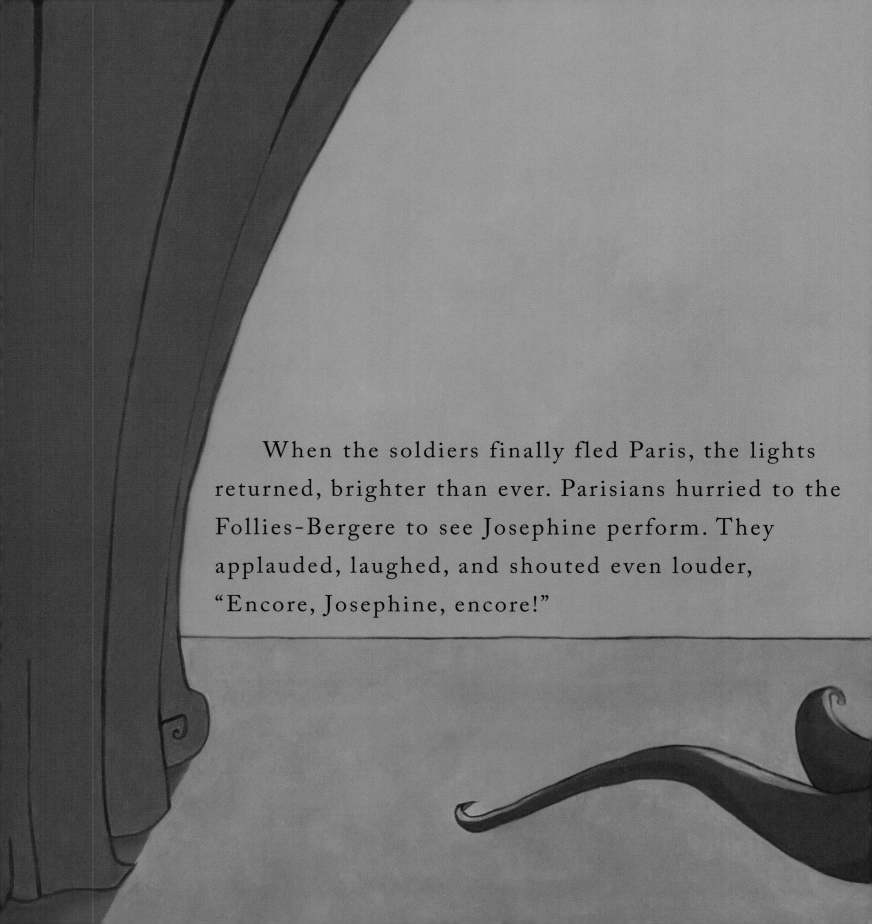

When the soldiers finally fled Paris, the lights
returned, brighter than ever. Parisians hurried to the
Follies-Bergere to see Josephine perform. They
applauded, laughed, and shouted even louder,
"Encore, Josephine, encore!"

The president of France presented Josephine with a medal of honor. He said, "Josephine, your singing is glorious, your dancing is magnifique, and your crazy funny faces are so droll. But best of all you helped us to get rid of the enemy. You brought light and color back to France."

Josephine bought a big house near Paris in a town called Les Milandes. She filled it with animals—Ethel the chimpanzee, Kiki the snake, and a leopard named Chiquita. But something was still missing. "My dreams came true," she said. "Now I need to help other children's dreams come true."

Josephine adopted twelve children. They were every color people can be. She brought them to live with her in Les Milandes.

Josephine called her family, "My Rainbow Tribe." To Josephine they were brighter than the lights of Paris. She sang for them and danced and made crazy, funny faces. Her children applauded and laughed and shouted, "Encore, Maman, encore!"

Josephine had many things. She had clothes
and jewels. She had animals enough for a zoo.
She had lights, applause, and laughter, and even
a medal of honor.

But nothing was more precious to Josephine
than her Rainbow Tribe.

"My biggest dream came true," she told them.

"What was that Maman?"

She held them close and whispered—"You."

AFTERWORD

Freda Josephine Carson became Josephine Baker, the toast of Paris.

She was talented, generous, openhearted, glamorous, intelligent, and funny—and not afraid to stand up for what she believed in. She and her Jewish husband, Jean Lion, belonged to an organization that fought against racism and anti-Semitism.

For her services to France during WWII, she was not only awarded the Medal of the Resistance with Rosette, but was also named a Chevalier of the Legion of Honor.

Josephine and her Rainbow Tribe taught the world that people of all races and religions could get along as family.

Josephine lived in France but never stopped loving America. She still performed in the country of her birth but refused to appear at segregated clubs and theaters. If blacks could perform on stage, she decided, they should also be allowed to sit in the audience! Josephine helped break down racial barriers. She even spoke at a rally alongside Martin Luther King.

Josephine Baker died in April 1975. Thousands of people crowded into the streets of Paris to watch the funeral procession. The French government honored her with a twenty-one-gun salute. It was their way of saying thank you to Josephine for her bravery during the war, and for the many years she made audiences applaud, laugh, and shout, "Encore, Josephine! Encore!"